W9-BVR-614

Date: 6/20/11

BR HILLERT
Hillert, Margaret.
Dear dragon's A is for Apple /

PALM BEACH COUNTY
LIBRARY SYSTEM
3650 SUMMIT BLVD.
WEST PALM BEACH, FL 33406

A Beginning-to-Read Book

Dear Dragon's A is for Apple

by Margaret Hillert
Illustrated by David Schimmell

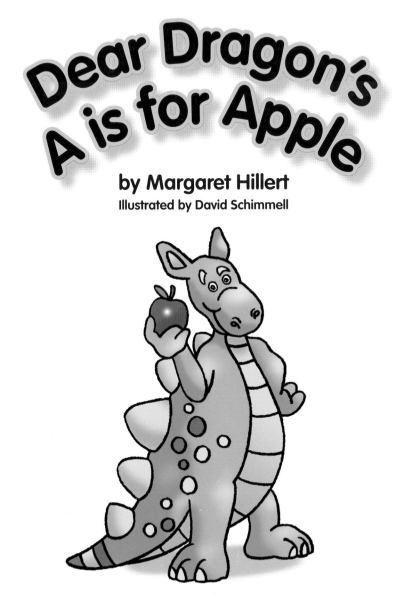

NORWOOD HOUSE PRESS

DEAR CAREGIVER,

The *Beginning-to-Read* series is a carefully written collection of readers, many of which you may remember from your own childhood. This book, *Dear Dragon's A is for Apple*, was written over 30 years after the first *Dear Dragon* books were published. The *New Dear Dragon* series features the same elements of the earlier books, such as text comprised of common sight words. These sight words provide your child with ample practice reading the words that appear most frequently in written text. The many additional details in the pictures enhance the story and offer the opportunity for you to help your child expand oral language skills and develop comprehension.

Begin by reading the story to your child, followed by letting him or her read familiar words and soon your child will be able to read the story independently. At each step of the way, be sure to praise your reader's efforts to build his or her confidence as an independent reader. Discuss the pictures and encourage your child to make connections between the story and his or her own life. At the end of the story, you will find reading activities and a word list that will help your child practice and strengthen beginning reading skills.

Above all, the most important part of the reading experience is to have fun and enjoy it!

Shannon Cannon

Shannon Cannon,
Literacy Consultant

Norwood House Press • P.O. Box 316598 • Chicago, Illinois 60631
For more information about Norwood House Press please visit our website at *www.norwoodhousepress.com* or call 866-565-2900.

Text copyright ©2008 by Margaret Hillert. Illustrations and cover design copyright ©2008 by Norwood House Press, Inc. All rights reserved. No part of this book may be reproduced or utilized in any form or by any means without written permission from the publisher.
Designer: The Design Lab

LIBRARY OF CONGRESS CATALOGING-IN-PUBLICATION DATA
    Hillert, Margaret.
    Dear dragon's A is for Apple / Margaret Hillert ; illustrated by David Schimmell.
        p. cm. — (A beginning-to-read book)
    Summary: "A boy and his pet dragon learn their ABCs"—Provided by publisher.
    ISBN-13: 978-1-59953-158-8 (library edition : alk. paper)
    ISBN-10: 1-59953-158-5 (library edition : alk. paper) [1.
Dragons—Fiction. 2. Alphabet.] I. Schimmell, David, ill. II. Title.
PZ7.H558Dej 2008
[E]—dc22   2007037020

Manufactured in the United States of America in North Mankato, Minnesota.
182R—042011

Here is something good.
Something that is
fun to look at.

3

Aa

apple

See the <u>apple</u>.
The <u>apple</u> is red.
It is good to eat.

Bb

balloon

Here is a <u>balloon</u>.
A big <u>balloon</u>.
It is fun to play with.

Cc

clown

See the <u>clown</u>.
The <u>clown</u> is funny.
He can do funny things.

Dd

This is a <u>duck</u>.
A little baby <u>duck</u>.
The <u>duck</u> is yellow.

duck

egg

Ee

Look at the <u>egg</u>.
The <u>egg</u> is little.
It is white.

Ff

fire

Here is a <u>fire</u>.
A red and yellow <u>fire</u>.
A <u>fire</u> is not to play with.

Gg

glasses

Look at the <u>glasses</u>.
Do you have <u>glasses</u>?
<u>Glasses</u> help you see.

Hh

horse

Here is a <u>horse</u>.
The <u>horse</u> is big.
The <u>horse</u> can jump.

ice cream

Look at the <u>ice cream</u>.
How good it looks!
<u>Ice cream</u> is good to eat.

Jj

jack o' lantern

This is a <u>jack o' lantern</u>.
The <u>jack o' lantern</u> is orange.
How funny it is!

Kk

kangaroo

Look at the mother <u>kangaroo</u>.
It can jump, jump, jump.
See the baby <u>kangaroo</u>, too.

Ll

leaf

Here is a <u>leaf</u>.
It is a pretty <u>leaf</u>.
It will come down, down.

Mm

monkey

See the <u>monkey</u>.
The funny, funny <u>monkey</u>.
Look what he can do.

Nn
numbers

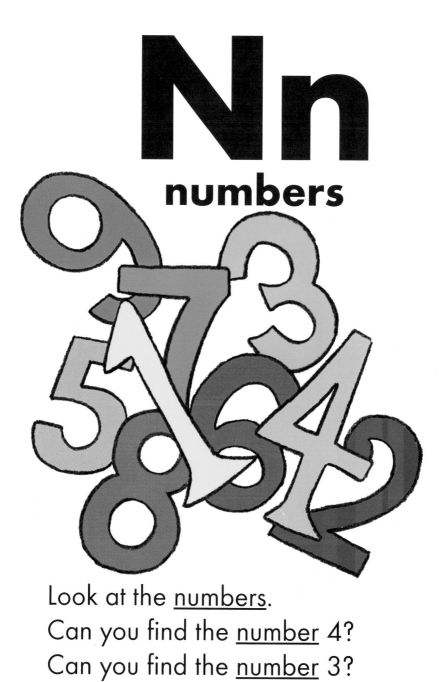

Look at the <u>numbers</u>.
Can you find the <u>number</u> 4?
Can you find the <u>number</u> 3?

Oo

owl

This is an <u>owl</u>.
Who? Who is it?
It is a little <u>owl</u>.

Pp

popcorn

Here is <u>popcorn</u>.
POP! POP! POP!
It is fun to make <u>popcorn</u>.

Qq

See the <u>quilt</u>.
The <u>quilt</u> is pretty.
The <u>quilt</u> is red and
blue and yellow.

quilt

Rr

rainbow

Look at the <u>rainbow</u>.
The <u>rainbow</u> is up, up.
How pretty it is!

Ss

school

Here is a <u>school</u>.
We like to go to <u>school</u>.
We have fun here.

Tt

tiger

This is a <u>tiger</u>.
The <u>tiger</u> looks like a cat.
A big, big cat.

Uu

umbrella

See the <u>umbrella</u>.
What a pretty <u>umbrella</u>!
An <u>umbrella</u> is good to have.

Vv

vegetables

Here are <u>vegetables</u>.
<u>Vegetables</u> are good to eat.
<u>Vegetables</u> are good for us.

Ww

witch

Oh, my!
Look at the <u>witch</u>!
The <u>witch</u> is up, up, up.

X x

x-ray

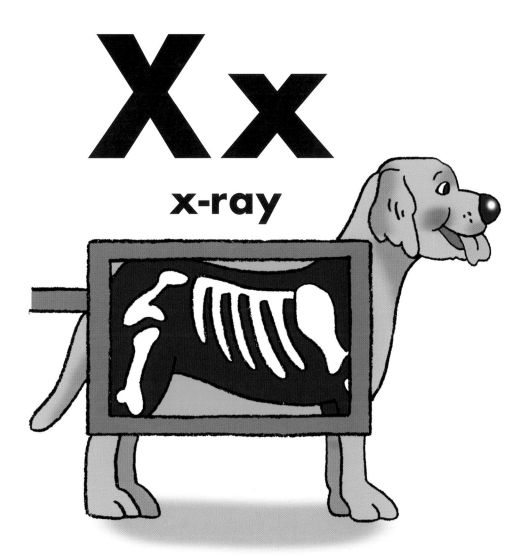

This is an <u>x-ray</u>.
An <u>x-ray</u> is good.
It can help you.

Yy

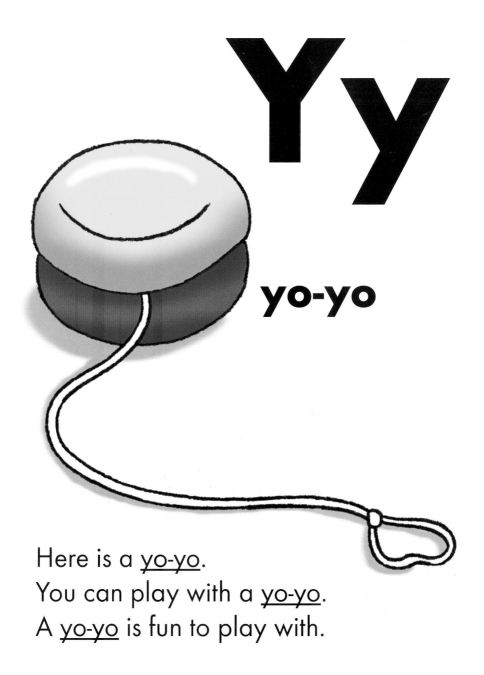

yo-yo

Here is a <u>yo-yo</u>.
You can play with a <u>yo-yo</u>.
A <u>yo-yo</u> is fun to play with.

Zz

zebra

This is a <u>zebra</u>.
It is black and white.
The <u>zebra</u> looks like a pony.

Aa Bb Cc Dd Ee Ff

Here you are with me.
And here I am with you.
Oh, what a good book,
dear dragon.

Gg Hh Ii Jj
Kk Ll Mm Nn
Oo Pp Qq Rr
Ss Tt Uu Vv

Ww Xx Yy Zz

READING REINFORCEMENT

The following activities support the findings of the National Reading Panel that determined the most effective components for reading instruction are: Phonemic Awareness, Phonics, Vocabulary, Fluency, and Text Comprehension.

Phonemic Awareness: The variant vowel /o͞o/ and /o͝o/

Oral Blending: Say the word parts below for your child. Say each word part separately. Ask your child to say the new word made by blending the beginning, middle and ending word parts together:

l + ook = look	bal + loon = balloon	g + ood = good
t + oo = too	b + ook = book	kang + a + roo = kangaroo
f + oot = foot	c + ook = cook	t + ool = tool
sp + oon = spoon	sh + ook = shook	w + ood = wood
p + ool = pool	h + ood = hood	t + ooth = tooth

Phonics: The letters O and o

1. Demonstrate how to form the letters **O** and **o** for your child.

2. Have your child practice writing **O** and **o** at least three times each.

3. Write down the following words, with spaces, and ask your child to complete each word by adding the letters **O** and **o** in the spaces:

n _ _ n	b _ _ k	sch _ _ l	h _ _ k	c _ _ l
f _ _ d	h _ _ d	shamp _ _	c _ _ kie	g _ _ se
s _ _ n	w _ _ l	cr _ _ k	sm _ _th	z _ _

4. Ask your child to read each word.

5. Help your child sort the words by the variant vowel sounds. (For example, sort words that have the /o͞o/ sound, like in moon, together and the words that have the /o͝o/ sound, like in cook, together.)

Vocabulary: Adjectives and Nouns

1. Explain to your child that words that describe something are called adjectives.

2. Write the following adjectives from the story on index cards and ask your child to read them and name something they might describe:

fun	good	big	funny
little	white	pretty	orange

3. After reading the story, provide your child with additional index cards labeled with the following nouns from the story:

jack o' lantern	clown	horse	leaf
rainbow	duck	balloon	book
monkey	apple	egg	

4. Help your child match the adjectives with the appropriate nouns. (Note: some adjectives will have more than one matching noun.)

Fluency: Echo Reading

1. Reread the story to your child at least two more times while your child tracks the print by running a finger under the words as they are read. Ask your child to read the words he or she knows with you.

2. Reread the story, stopping after each sentence or page to allow your child to read (echo) what you have read. Repeat echo reading and let your child take the lead.

Text Comprehension: Discussion Time

1. Ask your child to recite the alphabet and name as many alphabet words as he or she can remember from the book.

2. To check comprehension, ask your child the following questions:

   - What are the things you can eat in the book?
   - What things in the book make us laugh?
   - Why does the book tell us not to play with a fire?
   - What is the first letter in your name? Can you think of other things that start with that letter?

WORD LIST

Dear Dragon's A is for Apple uses the 93 words listed below.

26 words represent the letters of the alphabet and serve as an introduction to new vocabulary while 67 words are pre-primer. This list can be used to practice reading the words that appear in the text. You may wish to write the words on index cards and use them to help your child build automatic word recognition. Regular practice with these words will enhance your child's fluency in reading connected text.

Pre-Primer Words

a	dear	here	not	this
am	do	how		to
an	down		oh	too
and	dragon	I	orange	
are		is		up
at	eat	it	play	us
			pony	
baby	find	jump	pop	we
big	for		pretty	what
black	fun	like		white
blue	funny	little	red	who
book		look(s)		will
	go		see	with
can	good	make	something	
cat		me		yellow
come	have	mother	that	you
	he	my	the	
	help		things	

New Vocabulary Words

apple	owl
balloon	popcorn
clown	quilt
duck	rainbow
egg	school
fire	tiger
glasses	umbrella
horse	vegetables
ice cream	witch
jack o'lantern	x-ray
kangaroo	yo-yo
leaf	zebra
monkey	
numbers	

ABOUT THE AUTHOR Margaret Hillert has written over 80 books for children who are just learning to read. Her books have been translated into many different languages and over a million children throughout the world have read her books. She first started writing poetry as a child and has continued to write for children and adults throughout her life. A first grade teacher for 34 years, Margaret is now retired from teaching and lives in Michigan where she likes to write, take walks in the morning, and care for her three cats.

Photograph by Glenna Washburn

ABOUT THE ADVISER Shannon Cannon contributed the activities pages that appear in this book. Shannon serves as a literacy consultant and provides staff development to help improve reading instruction. She is a frequent presenter at educational conferences and workshops. Prior to this she worked as an elementary school teacher and as president of a curriculum publishing company.